Bernie Works
a Miracle

Leon Rosselson and Kate Sheppard

A & C Black · London

JUMBO JETS

Published 1992 by A&C Black (Publishers) Ltd,
35 Bedford Row, London WC1R 4JH
Reprinted 1994

ISBN 0-7136-3658-0

A CIP catalogue record for this book
is available from the British Library

Filset by Rowland Phototypesetting Ltd,
Bury St Edmunds, Suffolk
Printed in Great Britain by
William Clowes Ltd, Beccles and London

 I'm Bernie's best friend. Her real name's Bernadette but she won't let any of the children call her that.

Bernadette was some boring saint and I'd rather not have anything to do with her, thank you very much.

Sometimes a boy who thinks he's tough will call her Bernadette just to tease her and annoy her. Then he'd better watch out. If Bernie catches him, she'll bunch her right hand into a fist, raise it high in the air and bring it down hard like a hammer on his head. That usually puts a stop to that, because it hurts.

3

I know, because she did it to me once. It was one playtime when she told me I was her best friend.

Do I have to be?

I decided that, after all, if she said so, I probably was. Her best friend, that is.

'What does your best friend have to do?' I asked.

Share sweets, chocolates, crisps & peanut butter sandwiches & walk with me to school.

4

Actually, there are advantages to being Bernie's best friend. Now, nobody would dare to pull my hair or lift up my dress to see what colour knickers I'm wearing, or do anything stupid like that. They know that if they did, it would be hammer-on-the-head time.

We make a right pair walking to school.
I'm quite small, you see, and neatly
dressed. And my face is washed and my
hair properly combed and I have a sweet
smile, or so my mum says, which is
probably why I never get into any
trouble.

And Bernie is tall. She's very tall, taller
than any of the other children in the class.
In fact, if there was a tallest-girl-in-the-
world competition, she'd probably win it.

It's not only because she's tall that she looks so funny. She dresses oddly as well. Nothing seems to fit and she always wears big black boots which our teacher says are not at all suitable for a girl. I think that's may be why she's always getting into trouble – because of the way she looks. Whatever the reason, Bernie and school don't seem to get on very well.

HAY FOR HAIR

SLEEVES TOO SHORT

WHERE'S THE OTHER SOCK?

WOW, SHE'S TALL!

BIG BLACK BOOTS

7

Sometimes I think that she's accident-prone and sometimes I think she does it on purpose but either way, Bernie is trouble – serious trouble.

Once, she got into so much trouble that if there'd been a world getting-into-trouble competition, she'd have won it easily.

This is how it happened.

CHAPTER TWO

It was December, time for the nativity play, and I was chosen to play the Virgin Mary. That was the first problem. Bernie thought she should have been the Virgin Mary.

You're just a little too tall to be the Virgin Mary, Bernadette,

explained Mr Lawrence, who was rehearsing us.

Well, how tall was she, then?

She was annoyed. I can always tell when Bernie's annoyed because she clenches both her fists and her face fills with frowns. I just hoped she wasn't going to do anything silly and get herself thrown out of the play.

I'm not sure if the gospels are very specific on the matter of Mary's height.

'Nevertheless,' said Mr Lawrence, 'I do feel that for the purposes of this production, we need a small, innocent-looking Mary, which, with the best will in the world, you are not. However, we do need a shepherd who, I would say, is exactly your height. Yes, you'll make a very fine shepherd.'

I think he was trying to be sarcastic but you can never tell with Mr Lawrence. He has this way of speaking which makes you feel a bit stupid.

Anyway, Bernie seemed to accept the idea of being a very fine shepherd. But the next problem was that she absolutely refused to be 'sore afraid'.

'You've got to be,' said Mark, who was acting the angel of the Lord. 'I'm the angel of the Lord and you're just a shepherd and when you see me you've got to be sore afraid.'

YAWN

Mr Lawrence wasn't pleased. I could hear in his voice that he was losing his patience. 'I don't think we need you to rewrite the gospels, Bernadette. They've been good enough for most people for 2000 years.'

And lo the angel of the Lord came upon them and the glory of the Lord shone round about them: AND THEY WERE SORE AFRAID

Luke Chapter 2, Verse 9.

Now are you going to play the part as written or do we have to find ourselves a more co-operative shepherd?

CHAPTER THREE

'It's all your fault,' Bernie said as we were walking to school the next morning. 'You and your sweet smile.'

'I can't help having a sweet smile,' I said. 'It's the way I am. Like you can't help being tall.'

'What's wrong with being tall?' said Bernie, frowning and clenching her fists.

15

'Anyway,' I said, changing the subject as quickly as I could, 'I never wanted to be the Virgin Mary. It's a boring part. All I do is stand around smiling like some soppy doll. I'd much rather be a shepherd.'

Bernie looked at me. 'Really?' she said. 'You're not just saying that?'

'Honestly,' I said. 'At least you get to *do* things, be sore afraid and journey to Bethlehem and everything.'

Bernie seemed to be thinking deeply about that as we walked on.

And she was.
Or, at least, she
tried very hard
to be. That was
the trouble. She
tried so hard to
be an enthusiastic
shepherd, it stopped
the rehearsal.

When the angel of the Lord appeared, the
other shepherds covered their faces with
their hands and knelt down.

Bernie threw her
hands up in the air
and let out a horrible SHRIEK
and made
terrified faces
as if she'd just
seen the spider
monster from
outer space.

18

Then she pulled at her hair, hurled herself onto the floor, banged the stage and moaned, 'Oh, oh, oh . . .'

until Mr Lawrence shouted at her to stop.

WHAT ARE YOU DOING, BERNADETTE?

'Can you please do it without all that throwing yourself about? The audience will think you're having a fit.'

I'm being sore afraid, sir, like you said.

19

But that's what I would do if I was a shepherd & I'd seen the angel of the Lord.

Bernie will argue. That's one of the things that gets her into trouble.

Mr Lawrence sighed.

We can do without the histrionics, Bernadette.

I thought this *was* history, sir.

HISTRIONICS

shouted Mr Lawrence. I was afraid he was going to explode.

Over-acting. Just do exactly what the other shepherds are doing. All right?

Bernie looked put out.

BORING

The next bit went all right. Bernie led the shepherds to Bethlehem and they all looked in adoration at the baby Jesus in the manger, wrapped in swaddling clothes.

21

Suddenly, there was an ear-splitting yell from Bernie.

Mr Lawrence put his head in his hands as if he'd got the most awful pain in his neck. 'One more disruption from you, Miss Fairley, and you're out of the play,' he said.

'But the angel of the Lord promised we'd see the baby Jesus, sir, and it's only a doll and it doesn't do anything and it's nothing like a baby . . .'

'Bernadette!' yelled Mr Lawrence.

'Yes, Mr Lawrence.'

Mr Lawrence stood up and took a deep breath. I could see he was trying to calm himself. When he spoke it was very thoughtfully and slowly as if he was explaining something to a lunatic or to someone who didn't understand English.

THIS IS A PLAY

Which means you are *playing* at being shepherds - you are pretending to be those shepherds who witnessed the miracle of the birth of Jesus two thousand years ago.

'The baby Jesus is not actually required to do anything and so can perfectly well be represented by a doll. What is important is that you use your imaginations. Use your imaginations so that for you, for this brief hour upon the stage, this doll becomes the baby Jesus and you become those shepherds filled with wonder and awe. If you can believe in it, then the audience will, too.'

25

CHAPTER FOUR

It was the day of the final rehearsal before the evening performance. Bernie was unusually silent as we were walking to school. She was obviously brooding. I skipped along beside her, trying to cheer her up and get her to talk, because a silent, brooding Bernie worries me.

27

'What sheep? I can't see any sheep.'

'That's what I mean,' said Bernie. 'How can we be proper shepherds if we haven't got any sheep to tend?'

It dawned on me what she was talking about. 'You've got those papier-mâché models.'

Bernie gave me a withering look. 'We need real sheep, that's what.'

'"While shepherds watched their flocks by night." That's what it says. Right? Not "While shepherds watched their papier-mâché models".'

'If we had real sheep to tend,' Bernie went on, 'we could be proper shepherds and really believe in the angel of the Lord and all that being sore afraid stuff. And then the audience would, too. I bet with real sheep everyone would be a trillion times more filled with wonder and awe.'

'No, they wouldn't,' I said, beginning to panic.

I mean, it's daft pretending to be shepherds with those stupid papier-mâché sheep. Anybody can see that they're not real. I've never seen shepherds tending papier-mâché sheep. Have you?

I had to admit I hadn't.

'Of course not. There'd be no point in it, would there? They don't do anything. What's the point of us having shepherd's crooks and sheepdogs if all we're looking after is papier-mâché? The audience is going to think it's ridiculous. They're going to laugh at us.'

'Sheepdogs?' I said. 'You don't have sheepdogs.'

'Well, we ought to have,' said Bernie. 'All shepherds have sheepdogs.'

I could see where this conversation was leading, so I tried to bring Bernie back to real life.

'I could do it,' she said.
'I'm good with animals.'

It's true. She is. She's got a scruffy looking mongrel that she's taught to sit up and beg and bring back sticks and things.

'I've got a plan,' said Bernie as we reached the school gate. 'We'll go to the city farm after school . . .'

'We? I'm not going.'

'Yes, you are. You're my friend so you've got to.'

She was right, of course. I didn't want to go but I knew in the end it wouldn't make any difference. She has ways of making you do things you wouldn't dream of doing by yourself.

The final rehearsal went really well. Mr Lawrence congratulated us all and especially Bernie. He said it was the most convincing portrayal of a shepherd he'd ever seen.

'Huh!' said Bernie.

But I could see she was secretly pleased.

Back here by six o'clock,

said Mr Lawrence, clapping his hands.

CHAPTER FIVE

After school, we went through the park, towards the city farm. They've got geese and rabbits, a donkey, ducks, an enormous turkey, a couple of goats and this sheep which is quite old and mangy and very tame.

'This is what we'll do,' said Bernie. 'There's always two people looking after the animals. You've got to do something to make them watch you instead of me.'

'What am I supposed to do?'

Bernie thought for a minute. 'Put your finger in the rabbit hutch and scream out that one of the rabbits is biting your finger and won't let go.'

'Suppose the rabbit does bite my finger and won't let go?'

'That'd be good,' said Bernie. 'You won't have to pretend then.'

I didn't much like the sound of this. But it's no use arguing with Bernie. 'And what are you going to do?'

Bernie reached into her bag and brought out a dog's lead and a bunch of lettuce leaves.

This sheep's crazy about lettuce leaves. It's like me and peanut butter. It'll follow me anywhere.

'What happens when the people on the farm notice it's gone?'

'By that time,' said Bernie, 'it'll be safe in my back yard.'

'You're mad,' I said.

'I'll only be borrowing it. They ought to be pleased I'm going to give their old sheep an important part in our nativity play. It might become famous. I bet not many sheep get to be famous actors.'

'I think,' I said, 'I think that if there was a maddest-girl-in-the-galaxy competition, you'd win first, second and third prizes.'

CHAPTER SIX

The notice on the gate said the farm closed at 4.30 pm, so we didn't have much time. There were some ducks and geese scrabbling about in the cobbled yard as well as the enormous turkey which stood there glaring at us. That turkey always makes me feel nervous, though Bernie doesn't seem to mind it.

The other animals were in sheds at the side of the yard. There was only one person on duty, a tall woman wearing red wellingtons. I knew her face but I couldn't remember her name.

Hello, we'll be closing soon. Have you come to see the animals?

'What a daft question,' Bernie muttered under her breath as she made for the shed where the sheep lived.

Meanwhile, I went off to the rabbit hutches. When I got there, I looked for the largest rabbit, a black and white one, and stuck my finger through the wire of its hutch. It took no notice but a few smaller rabbits gathered round to sniff my finger. When they saw I didn't have food, they lost interest and moved away.

40

I had to do it. What else could I do? I shut my eyes, took a deep breath and let out a blood-curdling scream.

The rabbits leaped into the air, scampered wildly away from me and huddled together in a distant corner of the hutch.

I heard the sound of footsteps running. What was I going to say? That I'd been attacked by a man-eating rabbit? It was ridiculous. Nobody was going to believe that. Then I had a brilliant idea.

She looked at me. I think my innocent-looking face must have impressed her because she came over and comforted me.

Then she spent quite a lot of time looking for the spider and explaining that spiders couldn't hurt you and there was nothing to be afraid of. So I thought I must have given Bernie enough time to kidnap the sheep. When I left the shed, Bernie was nowhere to be seen so I ran off home as quickly as I could.

CHAPTER SEVEN

We'd agreed to meet on the corner at quarter to six. Bernie had a dog's lead attached to the sheep in one hand and, in the other, a bunch of grass and lettuce leaves which the sheep was nibbling. What's more, her scruffy old mongrel dog was dashing here and there, sniffing at everything in sight.

I couldn't believe it.

'Didn't your mum tell you off for bringing a sheep home?' I asked.

'I left it in my back yard. I don't think she noticed. She doesn't notice much.'

'Well, someone's going to notice us if we walk to school like that.'

'We'll go through the back streets. Anyway, what if they do? I'm only taking my sheep for a walk. It's not a crime, is it? It's only a sheep. It's not a lion or a dangerous wolf. I've never heard of a sheep harming anyone, not like those rottenweilers.'

Rottweilers. And what's that doing here?

'That's Shep,' she said. 'My sheepdog.'

I gave up. We went
the back-street way to
school. I tried to
pretend it was normal
to be walking along
with a tall girl in big
black boots who was
pulling along a sheep
and waving a bunch
of lettuce and grass,
while a hairy mongrel
raced up and down
and scooted under
our feet.

Fortunately, it was dark and we didn't see anybody from school. The few passers-by we did meet looked a bit surprised and a few of them smiled, but only one woman actually stopped and questioned us.

Isn't that the sheep from the city farm?

'Yes,' said Bernie. 'They've lent it to us for our nativity play. I'm looking after it.'

'Really?' She looked doubtful. But then she shrugged and walked on.

'That was a fib,' I said. 'They didn't lend it to us.'

'Yes, they did,' said Bernie. 'We borrowed it so they must have lent it to us. One borrows, the other lends – that's one thing I learned at school.'

I told you it's no use arguing with Bernie.

We went into the school playground
through the back gate. Bernie tied the
sheep to a drainpipe and gave it the rest
of the grass and lettuce to eat.

'How will you get them on to the stage?'
I said.

'Don't you worry about that,' Bernie
replied. 'It'll be amazing. Everyone'll be
completely and utterly amazed.'

I didn't doubt it.

CHAPTER EIGHT

I didn't see much of Bernie before the play. I was too busy getting dressed and made up. But, if I live to be a hundred, I'll never forget what I saw during the play.

The first part of the play went brilliantly.
I remembered all my lines when the angel
Gabriel told me the glad tidings. Then the
choir sang *Once In Royal David's City* and
the scene changed to Bethlehem.

The innkeeper sent us to the stable and
Jesus was born while the choir sang *Hark
The Herald Angels Sing*. I was quite
enjoying it. Everybody was looking at me
and I hoped they thought I was being a
good Virgin Mary.

Then there was the shepherds' scene. The stage went dark and there was a scuffling noise as the shepherds came on opposite me and Joseph and the infant Jesus in Bethlehem. We had to wait there in the dark until it was our turn again. As the light gradually came up on the shepherds, the choir started singing.

While shepherds watched their flocks by night...

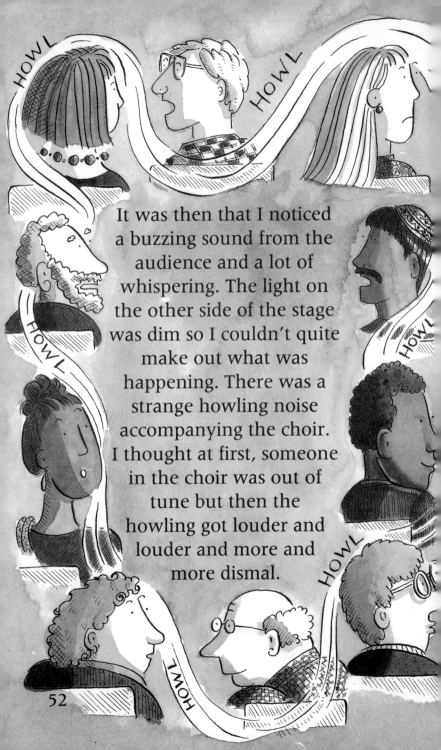

It was then that I noticed a buzzing sound from the audience and a lot of whispering. The light on the other side of the stage was dim so I couldn't quite make out what was happening. There was a strange howling noise accompanying the choir. I thought at first, someone in the choir was out of tune but then the howling got louder and louder and more and more dismal.

When the lights came up a bit more I could see Bernie's dog sitting in the middle of the stage with its nose pointed to the sky, howling for all it was worth. I thought it must have been in pain or maybe it just didn't like Christmas carols but whatever the reason, it was making the most eerie sound I'd ever heard. It made me want to cry.

HOWL

Then I saw Bernie standing alongside the shepherds. She was tugging at one end of the lead while the sheep tugged hard at the other. Sometimes Bernie pulled the sheep forward and sometimes the sheep pulled Bernie back.

The poor animal wanted to escape, I expect. And no wonder. By that time, so did I.

54

The choir seemed to be losing the battle with the howling dog. Some of the choir stopped singing and some half-stopped. Then those who'd stopped, started singing again at a different point from those who'd half-stopped until it got so confused, you couldn't recognise the tune at all. Eventually, the song petered out altogether.

The end of the song was the cue for the angel of the Lord to appear from the darkness at the back of the stage and be picked out by a spot-light which was supposed to be the glory of the Lord shining around. So when the singing died away, Mark thought it was his big moment. He danced to the front of the stage, tripped over the sheep's lead and fell flat on his face.

I know it's cruel, but this made everyone
on stage burst out laughing – even me.
Half the audience seemed to be laughing,
too, and the other half sat there frozen as
if they couldn't believe what they were
seeing. They were, I suppose, amazed, as
Bernie had said they would be. I didn't
dare look for Mr Lawrence. I thought
he'd probably have exploded by now.

56

When the shepherds saw the angel of the
Lord fall flat on his face, they decided
they had better carry on kneeling and
covering their faces and being sore afraid,
even though they were shaking with
laughter. Perhaps that's why Bernie let go
of the lead.

The sheep started rushing frantically about the stage, looking for a way out and baaing desperately. It's funny because I'd never actually heard that sheep make a sound before. Bleat, bleat, bleat, it went. Baa, baa, baa. Some people in the audience began cheering it on.

Ten to one the sheep.

BOO

Then Bernie's dog decided
to join in, so he started
racing about the stage after
the sheep, yelping and
barking. By now, half the
audience were on their feet,
clapping and shouting advice.
It was chaos. Mr Lawrence
jumped on to the stage
and ran this way and that,
trying to catch the sheep
and the dog, which only
made things worse. I just
shut my eyes and pretended
as hard as I could that I'd
wake up in a minute and
be somewhere else.

Go for
it.

Just when I thought that if it didn't stop soon I was going to have to scream, a most wonderful thing happened. Bernie stood up and started to sing loudly and clearly in a voice like an angel's. It was *Silent Night*, her favourite carol.

Now Bernie does sing beautifully. She has the best voice in the class. And the sound of her singing had a magical effect. It was amazing. Almost like a miracle. Almost like Jesus calming the wind and the waves.

The sheep and the dog stopped racing around and stood there quietly so that Mr Lawrence could lead them off the stage. All of us on the stage fell silent as if we'd had a spell cast on us. And the audience gradually settled back into their seats to listen while Bernie stood straight and tall and proud and sent her voice soaring to the rafters.

When the song ended, the hall was completely silent. You could have heard a pin drop. After that we went on with the play as if nothing at all had happened.

But of course, it had. Bernie got into terrible trouble even though, as she tried to tell everybody, she'd saved the show. She had to explain to the headmaster why she'd borrowed the sheep from the city farm.

She had to apologise
to the woman at
the farm . . .

and to Mr Lawrence and to the
other children in the play.

63

She wasn't allowed to attend any Christmas parties at the end of term. But she didn't seem to mind. She didn't seem to mind any of that.

Bernie was so happy she'd have won the happiest-girl-in-the-world competition.

She said being in the play was the best time she'd ever had at the school, the best time of her entire life. I suppose she thought that, after all, she'd been what she'd always wanted: the star of the show. And, in a way, she was right.